WOOF TALES & BULLIES

(In a Nic of Time)

God bless you!
Carol Clark

WRITTEN AND ILLUSTRATED BY CAROL FOSTER CLARK

WestBow Press books may be ordered through booksellers or by contacting:

WestBow Press
A Division of Thomas Nelson & Zondervan
1663 Liberty Drive
Bloomington, IN 47403
www.westbowpress.com
1 (866) 928-1240

ISBN: 978-1-5127-3553-6 (sc)
ISBN: 978-1-5127-3554-3 (e)

Library of Congress Control Number: 2016904714

Print information available on the last page.

WestBow Press rev. date: 04/28/2016

WESTBOW
P R E S S®
A DIVISION OF THOMAS NELSON
& ZONDERVAN

"Come on, Hannah, show me what you can do!"

"Woof! That's Nic with a frisbee! Time with Nic is always great, but with Nic *and a frisbee,* it's even better!"

"Hey, girl, you make grabbing a frisbee look *easy!*

Look at you go! You're a shaggy, flying ball of fur!"

"Hold on, Hannah. Here come Buck and his buddy Jerome, the cool guys at school. If only I could be part of Buck's group . . .

Hi Buck! Hi Jerome!"

"Hey, Nic, that's a high flying dog."

"Thanks, Buck. Want to throw the frisbee for her?"

"Nah, not right now. We got some stuff that makes *us* feel like we're flying higher than your dog. Wanna try some?"

"That sounds like *drugs*!

Buck, that stuff's not good. It can cause all sorts of problems."

"Come on, Nic, I thought you were cool. I didn't peg you for worrying about someday problems when you can have fun right *now*. What do you say?"

"Uh, I don't know . . ."

"Look, Buck, Nic is chicken! Cluck! Cluck! Cluck!"

"Think it over, Nic. Jerome and I will be back and give you another chance—but if you chicken out, we'll make it real hot for you at school!"

"Yeah, we'll *fry* you, won't we, Buck? We'll tell everyone you're a wimp, and **you'll be smoked!"**

"Oh, Hannah, I'm doomed! What do I do, girl?

They'll be back. If I cross Buck and his buddies, any thought I had of being cool will go up in smoke.

They'll fry me like an egg in a skillet . . . then flip me out onto the ground.

I'm scared, Hannah. I know what's *right,* but Buck is tough and everyone follows him.

How do I stand up to those guys by myself?"

"WOOF! You don't!"

"Huh, Hannah, did you just talk?

You're . . . you're a dog. Dogs don't talk."

"Woof! In the Bible, God let Balaam's donkey talk when it was important. *This is important.* This is your decision moment—your *Nic of Time*. You're facing a hot situation just like three boys in the Bible."

"Boys? What boys, Hannah?"

"Woof! The boys had funny names, but Shadrach (Shad-rack), Meshach (Me-shack), and Abednego (Ah-bed-nee-go) **believed in God.** They lived in a strange land without their parents, and no one else around them believed in God. They were all alone."

"The country was ruled by the great King Nebuchadnezzar (Neb-uh-kuh-d-nez-er)—the most powerful king in the world. He was so powerful and so proud that he wanted to be worshipped like a god!

He built a HUGE *gold* statue of himself *ninety* feet tall—as tall as FOUR houses stacked on top of each other!"

"That's one tall statue, Hannah!"

"Woof! That's when the trouble started."

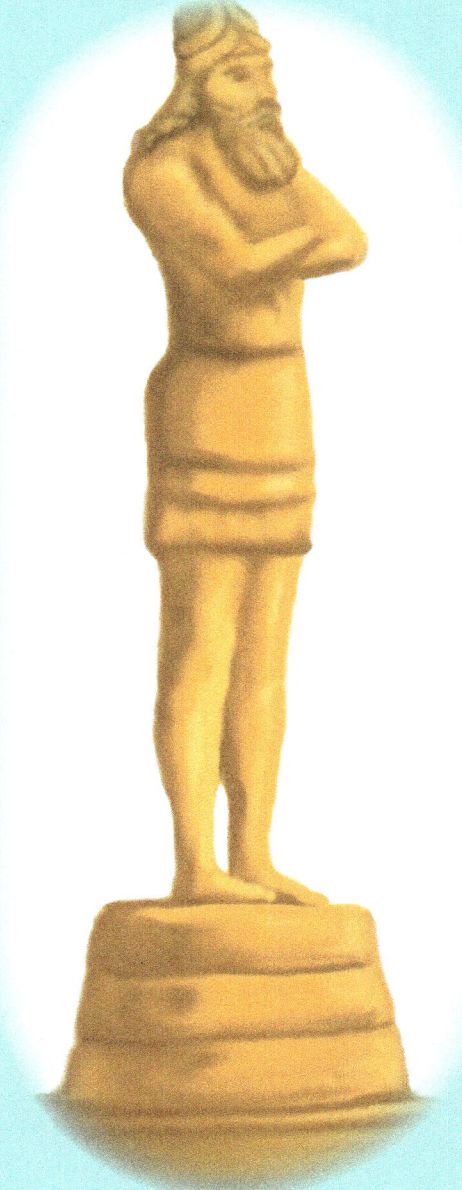

"The King had a big get-together to present his statue, and he ordered everyone in the country to be there. They all had to bow to the King's statue OR ELSE! Kings could do that. A king was the biggest bully on the playground."

"Hannah, the boys couldn't do that. It would be worshiping the King instead of God!"

"Yes, Nic, but the King said he would make it *really* hot for *anyone* who didn't buckle to his kneeling order. **He would throw them into a FIERY FURNACE!"**

"Oh, Hannah, what could they do? You don't live if you're thrown into a furnace!"

"Woof, you're right, Nic. Those Bible guys lived long ago and had funny names, but they were shaking in their sandals just like you are with Buck. They had to choose between God and the King. This was their *Nic of Time*. **Who would they choose?**

"But, Hannah, those guys were facing ***real*** death. With Buck, it just *feels* like I would die. What did they do?"

"Woof! They believed in God and decided they wanted to be **GOD'S GUYS.**"

"Woof! And when Shadrach, Meshach and Abednego refused to bend their knees, they were easy to spot.

You could say that they really STOOD OUT."

"Woof! The bully King arrested the boys and gave them one last chance, just like Buck and Jerome are giving you. Bow down and live, or refuse and *FACE THE FIRE!*

King Nebuchadnezzar roared, **'What God can deliver you from ME?'**"

"Oh, Hannah, how could three boys stand up to a King?"

"Woof! It wasn't easy, but Shadrach, Meschach, and Abednego bravely told the King, 'We know our God is able to deliver us, but even if that's not His plan, we still won't bow to your image.'

WOOF! God's guys chose the FIRE!

The King was **FURIOUS!** NO ONE defied HIM!
The angry King ordered his men to tie the boys up.
He ordered the fire to be made SEVEN times hotter!
Then he had his strongest soldiers throw them *into the flames!*"

"THE FIRE ROARED!

The flames were so HOT that the soldiers throwing the boys into the furnace were KILLED!"

"WOW, Hannah. *that's one hot furnace!* What happened to the boys? Brave is one thing, but DEAD is another. Is that the end?"

"Woof! The King thought it was . . ."

"The fire sizzled, crackled, and spouted flames!

The King listened for screams. He waited and waited, but he heard only the sputtering fire . . . and *silence.*

He stepped closer to peek into the furnace, but not *too* close because of the heat—and the dead soldiers.

Expecting to see burning bodies, *the King gasped,* 'D-d-didn't we throw *three* men into the fire?'

The people watching nodded their heads.

'I see FOUR!' the King exclaimed, 'They're walking around untied and unhurt, and . . . the fourth looks like the *Son of God!'*

Grrr! This King who wanted to be worshipped as a god knew a *real* GOD when he saw one."

"That's amazing, Hannah. Jesus, the Son of God, was right in the fire with them!"

"Woof! You're right, Nic!"

"The King called to Shadrach, Meshach, and Abednego. As the three boys stepped out of the furnace, everyone gathered around.

The King and the people stared. The boys were UNHARMED. The flames that *killed* the soldiers had only burned their ropes. *How could this be?*

The people crowded closer. They poked the boys' clothes, but they weren't scorched. They sniffed, but the boys didn't even smell smoky! They touched the boys' hair, but *not a single hair was even shriveled from the heat!*

The people and the King were shocked!"

"Woof! **The King knew REAL POWER when he saw it!**

He was more powerful than any king on earth, but he knew he didn't want to challenge this God.

The King proclaimed, ˈBlessed is the God of Shadrach, Meshach, and Abednego! He delivered them when they trusted Him, and when they chose to face death rather than bow to another god.

There is no other God that can deliver like this!'"

"Wow, Hannah, God's Guys didn't go into that fire alone. Jesus was with them!"

"Woof! Shadrach, Meshach, and Abednego bravely chose God and risked death!"

"You're right, Hannah. Here come Buck and Jerome, and I'm ready to face them now. If I give in to their bullying, I'd be bowing to Buck. I'm not going to bow to anyone or anything but God. I'm using my *Nic of Time* to choose God.

I want to be GOD'S GUY!"

"Woof! Good for you, Nic, and I know Jesus is with you because, just like Balaam's donkey,

I see things you don't."

WHAT WOULD YOU CHOOSE?

Would you stand for God or buckle to Buck?

Woof! Bullies may try to get you to do drugs, fight, cheat, steal, or pick on someone. What will you do with your *Nic of Time?*

Woof! Remember, if you choose to stand and take the heat, you won't be alone. Jesus will be with you.

When someone tries to bully you into doing something you know is wrong, be like Nic.

Choose to be GOD'S GUY or GIRL!

Woof! Visit my page at www.carolsartcorner.com. Click on Hannah's page.

CPSIA information can be obtained
at www.ICGtesting.com
Printed in the USA
BVOW07s0358230616

452895BV00015B/4/P